G.H.O.S.T. SQUAD

FRIGHT
at the MUSEUM

By K.A.Robertson

Illustrated by Katie Wood

Rourke
Educational Media

rourkeeducationalmedia.com

www.rourkeeducationalmedia.com

Edited by: Keli Sipperley
Cover layout by: Tara Raymo
Interior layout by: Kathy Walsh
Cover and Interior Illustrations by: Katie Wood

Library of Congress PCN Data

Fright at the Museum / K. A. Robertson
(G.H.O.S.T. Squad)
ISBN 978-1-68342-341-6 (hard cover)(alk. paper)
ISBN 978-1-68342-437-6 (soft cover)
ISBN 978-1-68342-507-6 (e-Book)
Library of Congress Control Number: 2017931186

Printed in the United States of America,
North Mankato, Minnesota

All cheer. No fear. That's the G.H.O.S.T Squad's motto. These girls hunting oddities and supernatural things are always up to something, whether it's cheerleading practice, pep rallies, or investigating spooks.

Mags, Scarlett, and Luna have built a business helping the haunted. And, along with Scarlett's service dog, Dakota, they're scaring up a lot of fun in the process. Each book in the G.H.O.S.T Squad series is self-contained, so they don't have to be read in any particular order. And every book is teeming with back matter, including an explainer section on paranormal studies, information about a real reportedly haunted location like that in the story, author interviews, and further reading suggestions.

Meet the Authors:
Brittany Canasi and K.A. Robertson have wanted to collaborate on a fiction series for years. And now they have! They worked together to develop the characters and concepts that drive the G.H.O.S.T Squad series, then they each wrote their books based on those ideas, helping each other shape their manuscripts along the way.

Meet the Illustrator:
Katie Woods' talent and commitment to bringing the G.H.O.S.T Squad characters to life were invaluable to the series. Katie is never happier than when she is drawing, and is living her dream as a freelance illustrator. She works happily from her studio in Leicester, England, and her work is published all over the world.

"The wonderful characters in this book have been an endless source of delight and inspiration. It has been so exciting to be part of the G.H.O.S.T Squad team and find out what adventures these girls will encounter next!" Katie says.

Brittany, K.A., Katie and the entire Rourke team hope these books tickle your funny bone and scare you silly!

Happy reading,
Rourke Educational Media

Meet the
G.H.O.S.T. Squad

*(Girls Hunting Oddities
& Supernatural Things)*

Luna: Discovered her psychic abilities in third grade, when a spirit warned her about the vegetables hidden under her pizza cheese. That night she also discovered her mother, a popular (and totally embarrassing) psychic on TV, is not psychic at all.

Other: Loves soccer and cheerleading. Hates broccoli.

Mags: Short for Magdeline. Her family has lived in New Orleans since it was founded in 1718. They know pretty much everything about everyone. And if they don't know, Mags knows how to dig up the dirt. Mags has a brain full of history knowledge and she's not afraid to use it.

Other: Best back tuck on the cheer squad. Afraid of clowns and pufferfish. (Don't ask why, she won't talk about it.)

Scarlett: Cheer captain, skeptic, and technology genius. Enjoys code cracking, hacking, and teaching her service dog, Dakota, strange tricks. Lost her left lower leg in an accident. Became gymnast and cheerleader soon after.

Other: Founded G.H.O.S.T. Squad in third grade after Luna told her about the invisible hero who saved her from a mouthful of greens. Still doesn't totally believe in ghosts. Still totally loves ghost hunting.

Dakota: Labrador. Scarlett's service dog. Recently learned to skateboard and sneeze on command. But not at the same time. Yet.

Other: Can smell ghosts. Will do anything for bacon.

Case ID: Weird1

Location: New Orleans Museum

Background: Famous romance writer's jewelry box collection on display. Odd activity observed since exhibit opened.

Reported Activity:

- Music boxes playing by themselves
- Typewriter sounds (no typewriters in building)
- Boxes in locked display cases switched overnight

Possible causes:

- Prankster?
- Spirit?
- Spirit prankster?
- Boxes grow arms, type novel set in boxing ring? On Boxing Day? Inside a box in a boxing ring on Boxing Day?

Hilarious, Scarlett!

Table of Contents

Chapter 1
Cooties

"Shhh. Listen. Did you hear that?" Luna whispered. She pulled Scarlett and Mags away from the crowd of students gathered around the museum tour guide.

"What? I don't hear anything," Mags said.

Scarlett put her hands on her hips and cocked her head to the side, eyes narrowed. "I don't hear anything, either," she whispered. "But, man, this place smells like old potatoes."

"Mike is talking about asking Bee to the school dance!" Luna whispered, grinning. She looked at Scarlett, then Mags. "What? Why are you looking at me like that?"

"I thought you heard a ghost," Mags said.

"Or something else exciting," Scarlett said.

"Well, Mike used to say girls have cooties and now he likes one, so that's weird and exciting, isn't it?"

"No," Mags said.

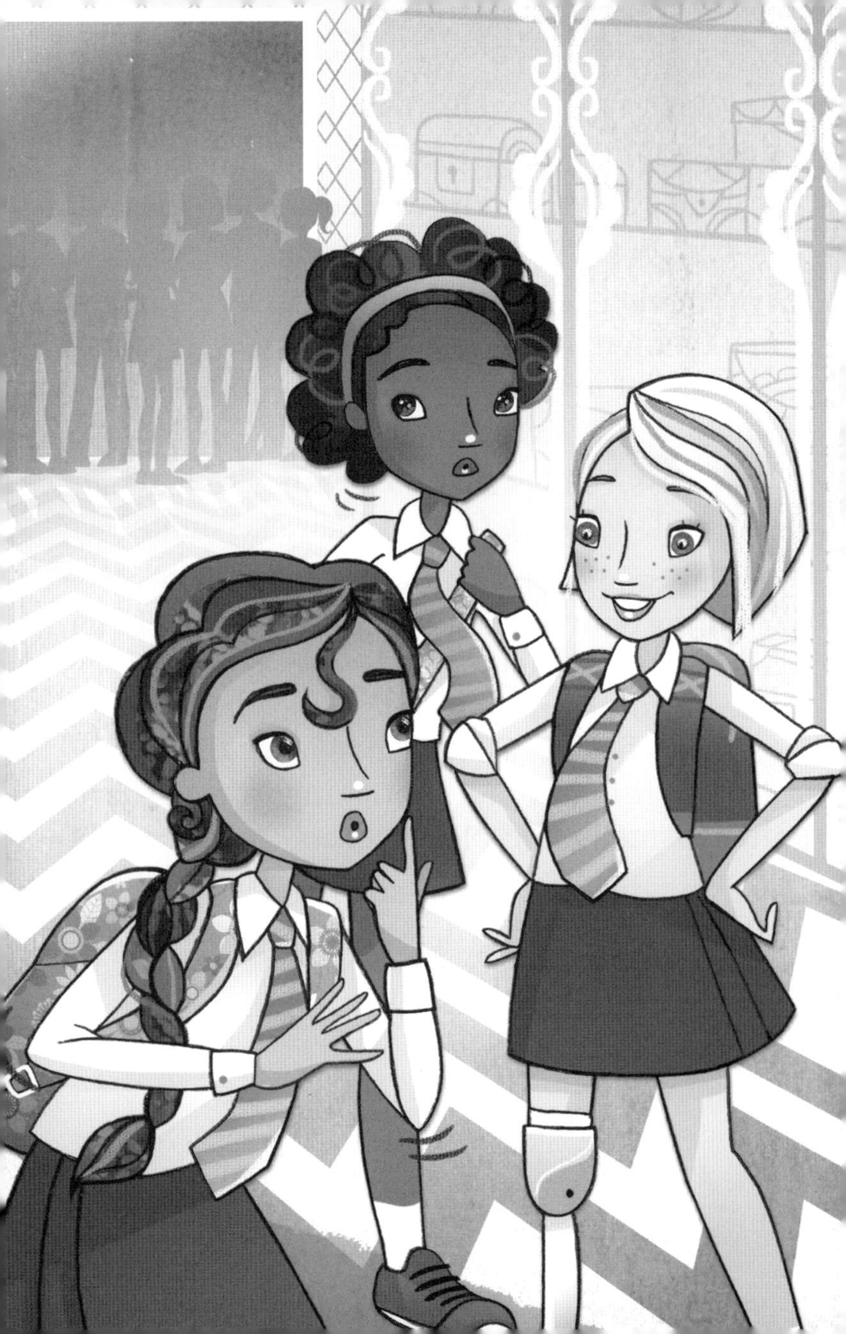

"Sort of," Scarlett said, seeing Luna's disappointed expression.

"Why do you know what old potatoes smell like?" Luna asked.

"Science experiment," Scarlett said. "I made potato batteries. I put them in my closet and forgot about them until my room started smelling like a crime scene."

"Gross," Mags said. "Hey, they're leaving," she said, pointing toward their classmates.

The gaggle of students began shuffling toward a door leading to another display. Luna, Mags, and Scarlett stayed back. This field trip had become a whole lot more interesting a few days before. That's when Mags discovered spooky things were happening in this (dark, dusty, smells-like-old-potatoes) room.

Now they were in it, all alone.

Chapter 2
A Few Days Before

SPOOKY THINGS HAPPENING IN OTHERWISE DULL PLACE

Boo! Is the local museum haunted? Staff members are freaked out by unexplained noises and strange occurrences among a recently acquired collection of jewelry boxes once owned by world-famous romance writer Parker Ramsey. The antique boxes were willed to the museum after she passed away earlier this year. In an interview before her untimely death, Miss Ramsey told *Writers are Weird* magazine that she began collecting the boxes as inspiration for her work.

"Jewelry boxes are designed to hold tokens of love," she said. "Each box has a story to tell. I make those stories up, since of course, the boxes can't speak. Though wouldn't it be lovely if they could?"

"I disagree with the headline. Museums are not dull," Mags said. She moved a stack of books off her bed and sat down next to Luna.

"Some of them are," Scarlett said. "The Pencil Museum was rather dull."

"That's a sharp criticism," Luna said.

"Are we done with the pencil jokes now?" Mags smirked.

"Yes. Forget I said anything. Erase it from your memory," Luna said.

"Luna, do you sense anything ... sketchy about this article?" Scarlett deadpanned. She looked down and pretended to flick lint off the "Some Assembly Required" t-shirt she was wearing. Mags and Luna had given it to her on her 10th birthday. It was faded and a bit snug, but it was still her favorite.

Mags rolled her eyes. Luna skimmed the article again. Then she closed her eyes for a few minutes. The other girls stayed quiet.

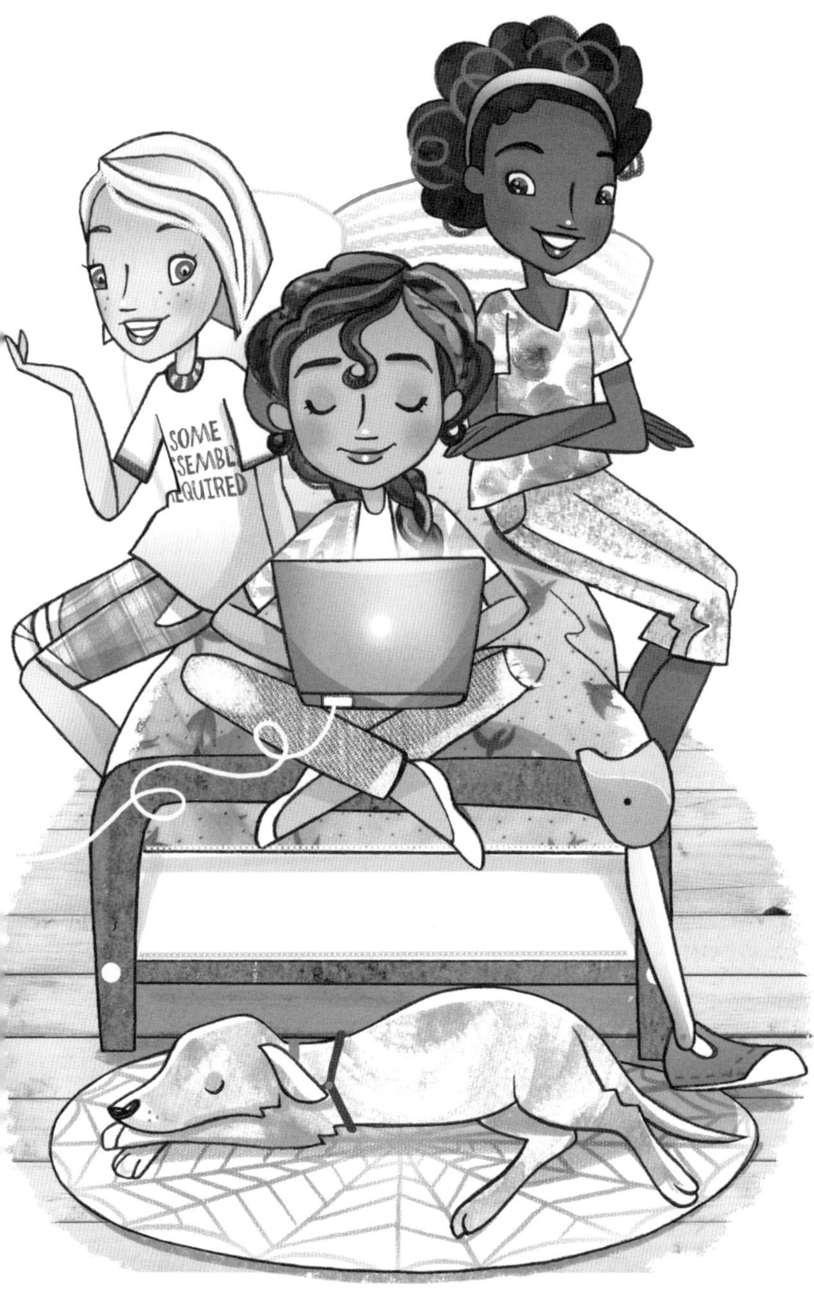
SOME
SSEMBLY
EQUIRED

Luna opened her eyes. Mags and Scarlett stared at her expectantly. "Well?"

"Well, I get a heavy feeling, heavy like *lead*, though I can't *draw* any conclusions from the spirit world," she said. (Mags groaned). "But I do think this should be added to the G.H.O.S.T. Squad docket. There could be something to it."

"Awesome. I'll pencil it in," Scarlett said, opening the investigation notebook and making some notes.

Mags groaned again. Luna snorted. Scarlett's phone chirped.

"Mom's looking for me. Gotta run," Scarlett said after reading the text. "Let's go, Dakota."

Dakota stretched and yawned, then picked up Scarlett's prosthetic leg and placed it in her lap.

"Good girl," Scarlett said, scratching Dakota behind her ears. She snapped her leg in place and stood up.

Then, Mags screamed.

"History Mystery is coming to New Orleans!"

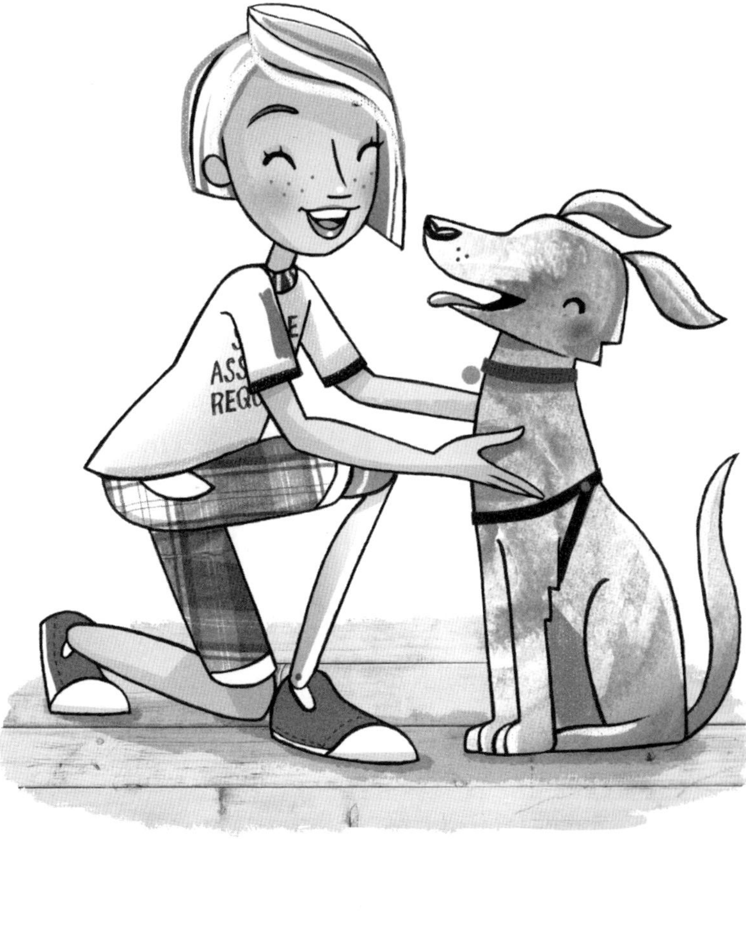

Chapter 3
XOXO

Luna and Scarlett closed the door to Mags' room behind them. Mags may not have noticed they left. She was still memorizing the details of her favorite show's filming schedule and plotting all the ways she could meet its host, Ben Bygone. And possibly become his co-host. She could see the headlines on *SMG* (Smart People Gossip) already:

Bright Young Star Stuns World With Amazing Brain and Killer Back Tuck!

Magnificent Mags Solves Mysteries, Makes History and Straight A's

Mega-Star Mags Takes Over History Mystery, World Becomes Smarter By Proxy

Buzz, buzz, buzz. Mags' phone vibrated in her hand, pulling her out of her daydream.

12,000,000 Chapters a night

 **Squad**

Scarlett:
Mags! Are you still screaming?

Mags:
No. Not really. Not out loud.

Scarlett:
OK focus! xo

Luna:
xo from me, too!

Mags put her phone down and sighed. *History Mystery* would have to wait. She had her own mystery to figure out for now. She opened her laptop and typed "Parker Ramsey" in the Zoogle search bar. A second later, she had thousands of results. Most of the top results were fan clubs. She also found the author's official website. She clicked on that one first.

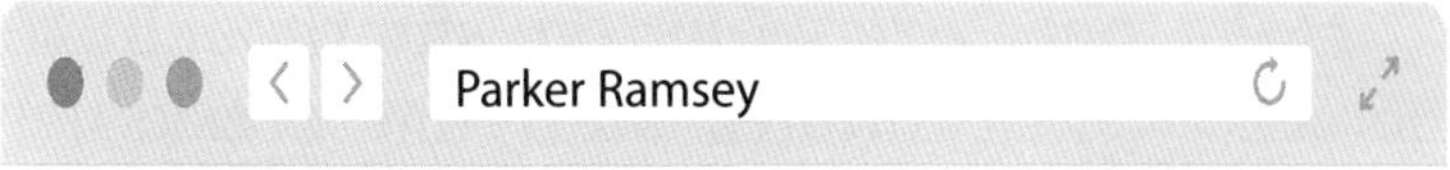
Parker Ramsey

Parker Ramsey, Romance Writer

Best-selling author of hundreds of novels, including:

Lost Love

Found Love
(the sequel to the worldwide sensation *Lost Love*!)

Lucky in Love

Not-So-Lucky in Love
(the sequel to the worldwide sensation *Lucky in Love!*)

Strange Love

Not-So-Strange Love
(the sequel to the worldwide sensation *Strange Love!*)

Parker Ramsey was born and raised in New Orleans, Louisiana. After her mother died, she lived with her grandmother, a voodoo priestess who specialized in love potions. Parker was fascinated by the stories she overheard her grandmother's clients share as they waited for their potions to brew. The love potions were placed in jewelry boxes once they were ready. Parker began collecting jewelry boxes as a teen, and used those boxes to inspire the romantic tales in her beloved novels.

Mags clicked on the word *boxes*, which led to a page dedicated to Miss Ramsey's collection. She zoomed in on each photo, looking for anything unusual.

Ugh, there are so many, she thought to herself twenty minutes later. She rubbed her eyes and stretched, then clicked back to the Zoogle results. She clicked on an article about the author's death.

Parker Ramsey

Famous Romance Author Dies Unexpectedly

Romance novelist Parker Ramsey passed away at her New Orleans home yesterday. Sources say she had a heart attack at her desk. According to authorities, there was one sheet of paper in her typewriter, and it appears to be the last page of a new book.

Miss Ramsey's agent reportedly ransacked the house looking for the rest of the pages. She found nothing.

"This was to be Parker Ramsey's greatest book yet," the agent said. Mascara streaked the woman's face as she bawled and sniffled in front of the news cameras outside the author's house. "Her death has cost us all dearly. Me especially," she said.

To: Luna, Scarlett

From: Magdaline

Subject: Voodoo, love potions, and missing pages

Hey,

Looks like Parker Ramsey died in the middle of writing a book. Her agent can't find the manuscript. Also, her grandmother practiced voodoo. I think she's the one my grandmother visited before she met my granddad. I would ask but I don't want to know the details.

Maybe she's come back to tell her agent where the book is?

~M

To: Magdaline, Luna

From: Scarlett

Subject: RE: Voodoo, love potions, and missing pages

Bonjour, mes amis! (studying for French quiz. Es-tu?)

Very interesting. What if it's Parker Ramsey's agent stirring up the trouble at the museum to get more people interested in buying her books? She makes money every time they sell, right?

Hugs,
S

To: Scarlett, Magdaline
From: Luna
Subject: RE: Voodoo, love potions, and missing pages

Scarlett, always the skeptic LOL. That's a great theory though. Let's keep an eye out for anything suspicious at the museum.

Gotta go, Mom's show is about to start. She needs me to run camera.
~ L

"communicated" with a ghost, Luna's mom placed an EMF meter on the table. She made a big show about demonstrating that it was not picking up any changes in the electromagnetic field. Then she closed her eyes, leaned her head back, and let her hands drop.

Luna knew her mom would pull the magnet from under her chair and place it under the table. Right below the EMF. The magnet made it spike. The spike made TV viewers think a ghost had entered the studio.

Luna's mom was like one of those talk show reporter ladies, if talk show reporter ladies interviewed fake ghosts. Luna used to feel sorry for the callers her mom was faking out. Then she found out most of the callers were fake, too. Just people calling with fake stories made up so they could be on TV.

That's why her parents didn't believe her when Luna said she could really see and hear spirits. Sometimes she even dreamed about things before they happened. Her family thought it was all in her imagination.

Luna was mad at first. Then a ghost told her where they hid the cookies meant for special occasions and other fantastic secrets.

She decided it was a good idea to protect her sources after that. If her parents knew she could get the goods on secret sweets stashes from a ghost, they might stop buying them altogether. Ghosts? Meh. A house without cookies? That would be scary.

"Luna, Earth to Luna!" her brother said, jabbing her in the ribs. "Show's over, turn that thing off."

Luna snapped out of the cookie daydream she'd been in for pretty much the entire half hour of her mother's program.

"That was great, Ma," she said. "Can we borrow the EMF meters for our field trip? We've got a possible case at the museum."

"Sure, sweetie. But you know —"

"I know, I know. 'There's no such thing as ghosts,'" Luna said.

"That's right, dear. Just make sure I get them back before next week's show."

"Will do. Thanks, Ma!" Luna kissed her mom's forehead. She ran up the stairs two at a time, wiping the forehead makeup off her lips. She loved her mom. She did not love the taste of sweaty forehead makeup.

"We, uh, got separated from our class," Mags said. It was mostly true. Mags hated lying. "And then the music started. We didn't touch anything, promise."

The music faded as they spoke. The woman sighed. Her breath was visible in the chilly air.

"It's the strangest thing," she said. "I've been the curator here for ten years. Nothing like this has ever happened before we opened this exhibit. My janitor quit last night after he found one of the boxes in the middle of the floor. He was the only one here at the time."

"We read an article about the weird stuff happening. It said people are hearing typing noises," Mags said. "Have you heard those, too?"

"I haven't, but my assistant has. Scared her out of her wits. We don't have any typewriters in the museum. I'm afraid she's going to quit soon, too."

"Ma'am, we may be able to help," Scarlett said. She handed a card to the curator.

The curator looked down at the card, then back up at the girls. "I've heard of you. Do you really think you can help?"

"We will certainly try," Scarlett said. "Can you tell me if Miss Ramsey's agent has visited

G.H.O.S.T. SQUAD
(GIRLS HUNTING ODDITIES & SUPERNATURAL THINGS)
ALL CHEER, NO FEAR
1 PSYCHIC, 1 SKEPTIC, 1 HISTORIAN
HAVE A HAUNTING?
CALL OR TEXT
999-999-9999

the collection since it went on display?"

"I'm not sure. Why?"

"Well, she seemed pretty upset about losing out on Miss Ramsey's last book, since the manuscript is missing. It's possible she might be trying to drum up interest in her other books by faking a haunting," Scarlett explained.

"I'm not sure how she would have gotten into the display cases. The boxes are in a different case every morning when I come in. I have the only key. Our janitor accused me of trying to trick him with the box. I had to FaceTime him to prove I was in my kitchen across town."

"Yikes," Mags said. "We might need to do an overnight investigation to get to the bottom of this." She didn't look happy about it. Mags much preferred sleeping in her own bed.

"Stay all night in the museum? I don't know, that's not something we ordinarily do," the curator said. "But, I guess these are not ordinary circumstances."

"We can come tonight after cheerleading practice," Scarlett said.

The curator nodded. "See you then."

Chapter 6
We've Got Spirit, Yes We Do

"S-P-I-R-I-T, S-P-I-R-I-T, spirit! Hey, let us hear it! Gonna high gear it! 'Cause we've got spirit!" the cheer squad chanted.

"Nice job, guys," Scarlett said. "Practice same time tomorrow."

Luna and Mags hung back while the rest of the team headed toward the locker rooms.

"Are you ready to ruuuuuumbleeeee?" Luna asked.

"Ready as I'm ever gonna be," Mags said.

"I'm ready," Scarlett said. "Mom said she'd bring Dakota and drop us all off at the museum in fifteen minutes. Wait until you see my latest invention!"

"What is it?" Mags and Luna asked at the same time. "Jinx!"

"I'm not telling. And now you're jinxed so you can't talk until we get there," Scarlett laughed.

The ride across town was anything but

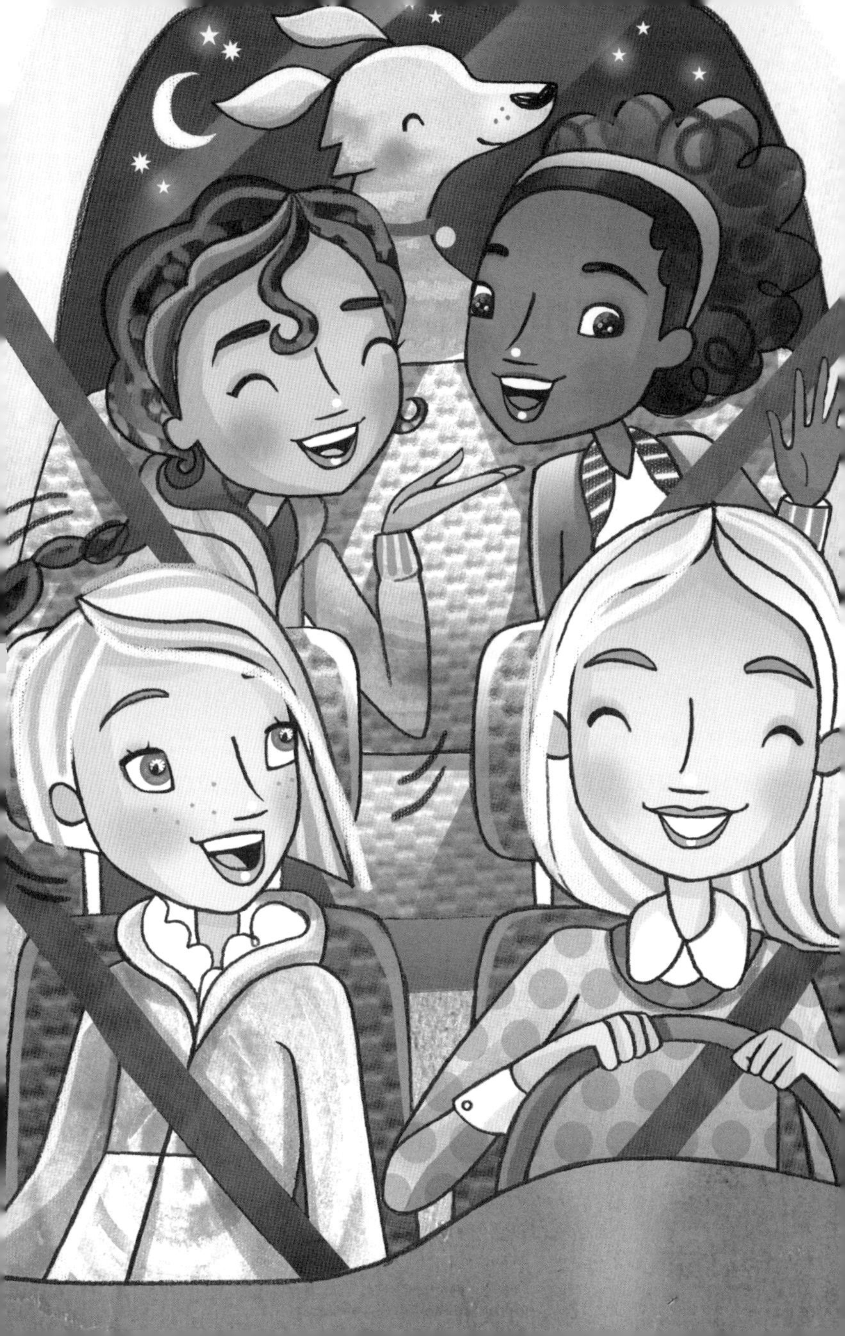

silent. Scarlett's mom blared the radio. The girls sang along. Dakota barked. It wasn't until they turned into the museum parking lot that the quiet settled over them like a fog.

"You girls sure you want to stay all night?" Scarlett's mom asked.

"Yes, Mom," Scarlett said, leaning forward to kiss her cheek. "We'll call you if anything changes."

"Like if a ghost chases us out of the building," Luna said, laughing.

"That is so not funny," Mags mumbled.

The curator opened the museum door before they could knock. "Come in, come in. I must go. I keep hearing those typewriters and I think I'm losing my mind. I'll be back in the morning," she said, rushing past the girls and down the stairs. "Good luck!"

"Sheesh. What's her hurry? She acts like she just saw a ghost," Luna said.

Luna and Mags laughed. The lights in the museum all blazed on at once.

Then, darkness.

Chapter 7
Weird

Boom! A loud bang shook the building.

"What was that? I can't see a thing," Scarlett said. She felt around in her backpack until her hand closed around a flashlight. Dakota growled low and creeped toward the middle of the museum. "Follow us," Scarlett said, beckoning with the flashlight.

"Listen," Mags said. "The boxes are playing again."

"Something … someone … is here," Luna said. "Or, they were a minute ago."

In the center of the room, one jewelry box stood in the middle of the floor, its top closed. The lids of the other boxes were open, their music still playing.

"Weird," Mags said.

Scarlett pulled a tablet out of her backpack. She quickly connected it to a small radio and a tape recorder. "I've tweaked the ghost box I made since we tried to use it last time," she said.

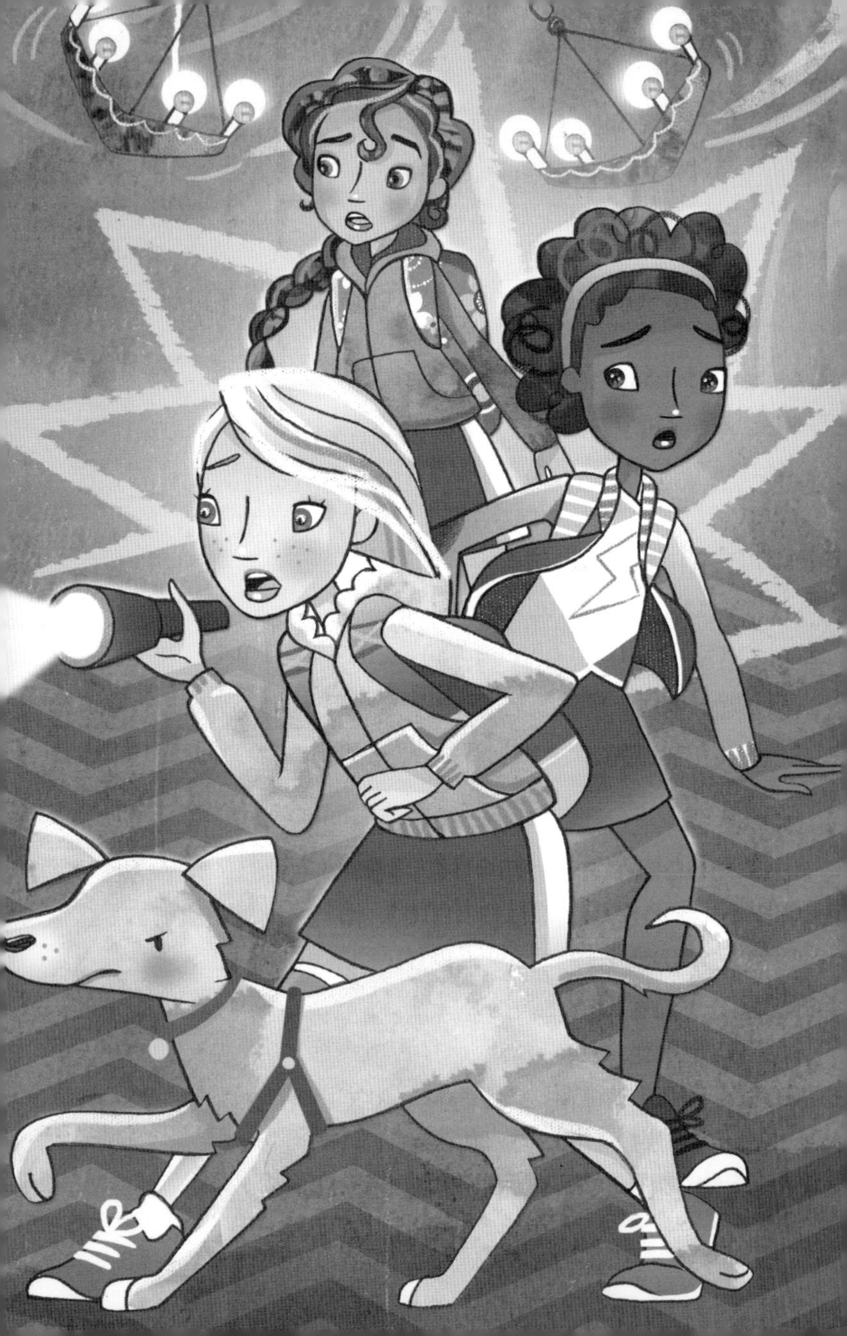

"You mean when it recorded the truckers talking on their CB radios instead of our investigation?" Luna asked.

"Yep," Scarlett said. "This time it will work. I think."

"I'm getting something," Luna said, pulling a notebook from her back pocket. The music quieted. The faint sound of clicking typewriter keys floated in the air. It was so quiet the girls couldn't tell at first if they were hearing it or imagining it. Dakota's hair stood up. She growled low, looking at the ceiling, then back at the closed box on the floor.

Luna scribbled on her notebook for a moment. Then she showed it to the others.

Stuck

Open

Music

Letter

Shoe Closet

"Shoe closet?" Mags said, making a face. "Weird."

"I wonder ..." Scarlett trailed off, staring quizzically at the ghost box she'd assembled. She hit play on the recording. Static filled the air. Then, a voice:

"Stuck. Open. Music. Letter. Shoe Closet."

"WEIRD!" Mags exclaimed. Luna and Scarlett looked at each other.

"Well, I guess it works," Scarlett said. "Or were you over there whispering into it while you were writing?"

"Of course not!" Luna said.

"Okay, okay. You know we have to rule out natural causes first," Scarlett said.

"Let's focus," Mags said. "Do you think the spirit is saying she's stuck here?"

"Maybe," Luna said.

Dakota sniffed the box on the floor, then put her paw on top of it. "Woof!"

The girls looked at her. "What is it, Dakota?"

"Woof!"

"Can you build a dog box that translates for her, please?" Luna asked.

38

Scarlett laughed. "I tried in second grade. It just made her bark sound like a duck quacking. Funny, but not helpful."

Mags dropped to her knees beside the box. She ran her hand along the edges.

"The lid is stuck," Mags said. "That's why it isn't opening like the others."

"Here, use this," Scarlett said, pulling a knife from her backpack.

"Uh, thanks. Why do you have a knife in your bag?" Mags asked.

"In case of a ghost attack," Scarlett said. "Just kidding, I brought it to cut our apples."

Mags ran the knife along the edge of the box, loosening the seal. Then she wound up the music key on the back. The lid popped open. A sad tune played while a tiny gold ballerina spun.

"Look, a drawer opened, too!" Luna carefully pulled the drawer from the box. A sheet of paper was folded inside.

"What's it say?" Mags asked, her eyes wide.

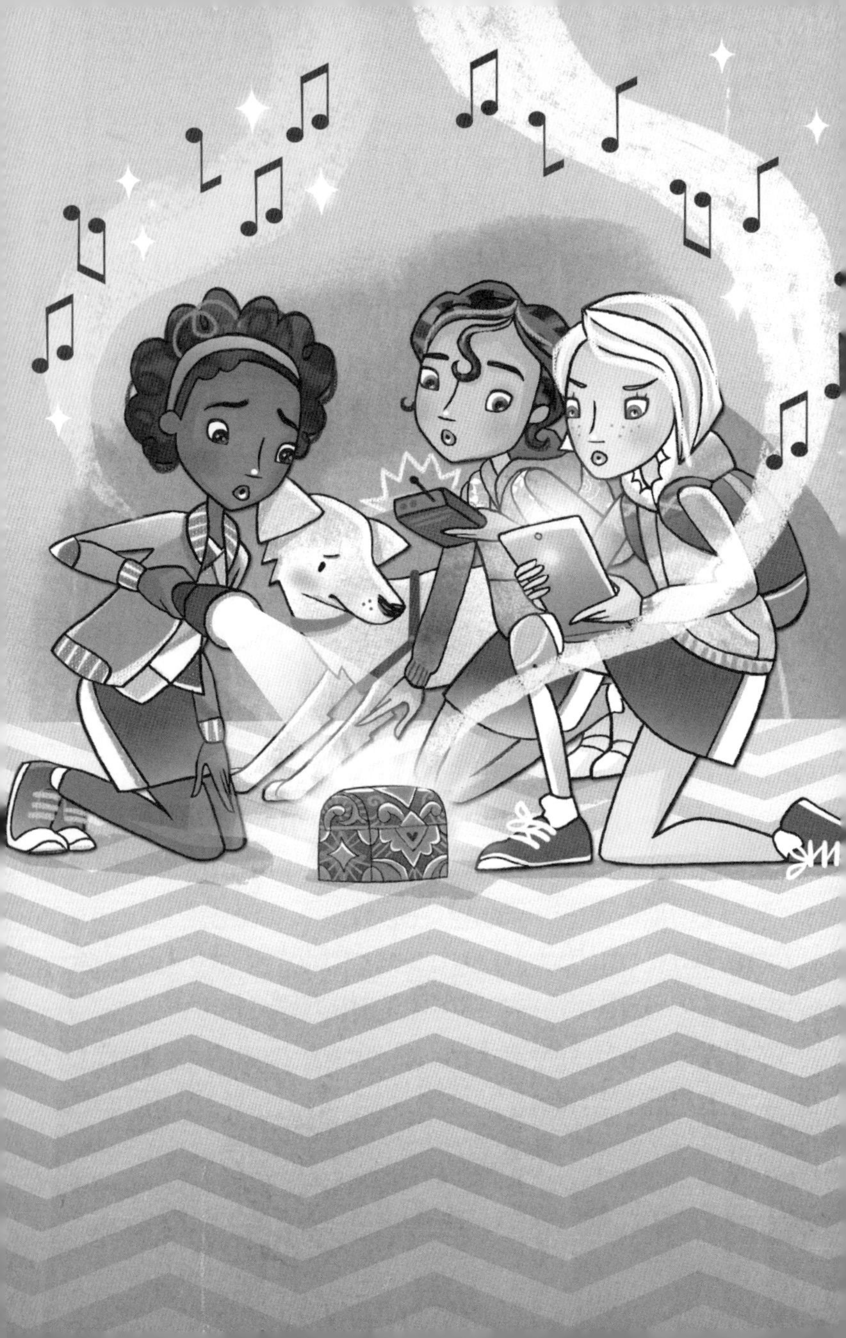

Dear Sir or Madam,

If you're reading this letter, I've passed on. Oh, dear, I hope I was wearing something lovely when it happened. I willed my jewelry box collection to the local museum, so I'm sure someone will find this note. If they don't, it will be simply awful! Alas, I must not think that way. I am quite certain it will be found right away. Where was I? Oh, yes. The purpose of this letter is to give you the location of my latest manuscript. I cannot be certain that it is finished, because I cannot be certain when I will cross over. It may not be very good, either. Most of them were stinkers, to be honest. That's beside the point. Any-hoo, the manuscript is under the floorboards in the hall shoe closet. Seemed a good place to hide it, yes? No one wants to go digging under smelly footwear! Except now, well, I guess someone must now do just that.

With love from beyond,

XO Parker Ramsey

Chapter 8
A Few Days Later

"The museum curator called," Scarlett said. "The activity has stopped since we gave her the letter."

"I wonder who had to dig under the pile of stinky shoes," Mags said. "I bet Parker Ramsey's agent is happy."

"I don't know about her, but you are about to be very happy," Luna said.

"Why? What? Are you having a psychic thing? What's going to happen, why am I going to be happy?"

Luna and Scarlett grinned at each other. They each took one of Mags' hands.

"Well, *History Mystery* also called this morning," Luna said. "They're going to film a segment on the haunted antique jewelry boxes."

"And guess who they want to be on the show?" Scarlett smiled widely.

"Us? Us? US?" Mags squealed.

"We solved the mystery, didn't we?" Luna said.

Mags squeezed her friends tight in a hug.

"Do you think they'll make me a permanent star on the show?" Mags whispered. "Luna, do the psychic thing. Find out if they will make me a star."

Luna pulled her Magic 8-Ball keychain from her pocket and shook it. "Signs point to maybe," she read.

Bonus Stuff!

What is Paranormal Research?

Something that lies outside normal experience or scientific explanation is considered paranormal. When people claim to sense or see ghosts, that is a paranormal experience. Science has not been able to prove the existence of ghosts. On the other hand, there's no conclusive evidence they don't exist, either.

Paranormal researchers are not necessarily scientists. Scientists have much stricter guidelines for performing experiments that can be tested and retested. Paranormal researchers use the tools available to them to collect evidence, such as electronic voice phenomena (EVP), and electromagnetic field (EMF) readings. They also rely on personal accounts of witnesses who think they are experiencing paranormal activity, and their own experiences in a haunted location. Researching a location's history is also a critical part of paranormal research. An investigator will gather information about the people and events associated with a place to determine if there is a reason for the paranormal activity to occur, such as a sudden death or a traumatic event. Proving the existence of a ghost in a way that can be tested and retested in a scientific manner is quite tricky, since no one's figured out how to catch one yet!

A "Real" Haunted Museum

It's been called the most haunted place in New York City. Set between residential buildings, Merchant's House Museum is said to be haunted by its former inhabitants, the Tredwell family. The Tredwells lived in the home from 1835 to 1933. Most of their furniture and other possessions are still there. The museum boasts a collection of 3,000 Tredwell family belongings, to be exact!

The home, now owned by the city of New York, opened as a museum in the 1930s. Since then, reports of strange sounds, sights, and smells are common occurrences. The unexplained experiences have spanned nearly a century! Apparitions, slamming doors and creaky floorboards spook visitors, staff, and volunteers alike.

To visit the museum, you must ring the doorbell. Once inside, you might be greeted by the spirits of siblings Gertrude, Elizabeth, and Samuel, or their father, Seabury. Visitors claim the spirits resemble the photos of the family members. The spirit of Gertrude, the youngest of the family, is said to be the most active. She died alone in the house at the age of 93, in the same bed in which she was born. Now, she is rumored to haunt the kitchen, glide up and down the stairs, rearrange dishes, and play the piano.

Merchant's House Museum offers candlelight ghost tours for visitors. And if you see or feel something, its staff invites you to share your experiences for their collection of ghostly lore.

Merchant's House Museum

What is a Medium?

In the G.H.O.S.T Squad series, Luna is described as a medium, or sensitive. This means she can tune into the energy of spirits around her, to feel their emotions and communicate with them. Not all people who claim to be psychic are mediums. Some psychics only claim to see into the past and/or future. A medium is defined specifically as someone who claims to communicate with the spirits of people who have passed away. Like ghosts, science hasn't proven these abilities really exist, but they haven't disproven their existence either.

Q & A with K.A. Robertson

Q: *Have you ever visited a psychic or medium?*
A: I have had two psychic readings. One of them told me some interesting things about my sons' futures. I'm still waiting to see if those predictions come true!

Q: *Why are you so interested in the paranormal?*
A: I've always been fascinated by things that can't be explained, and things that only exist in our collective imaginations. Unicorns, magic, ghosts, fairytale creatures — it's fun to think about things that are out of the ordinary, and spin stories around those things.

Test Your Reading Comprehension!

1. Why did Parker Ramsey collect jewelry boxes?

2. What did Parker Ramsey's grandmother do for a living?

3. What is Mags' favorite show? Why do you think she likes it so much?

4. Why was the jewelry box collection at the museum?

5. Mags, Luna, and Scarlett each have a specialty in the squad. What are their specialties?

Further Reading

For more information, check out your local library for books on ghost lore. Many books focus on specific regions. You may discover some haunts in your own hometown! You can also look for books on paranormal research and equipment such as electromagnetic field (EMF) detectors. If you're interested in a specific place that's rumored to be haunted, dig into public records and periodicals such as old local newspapers to see what you can find out about the people who once lived or worked there. Is there a mystery to be solved that might explain reports of a haunting? Try to solve it!